The Bold Kitten

Other titles by Holly Webb

The Bold Kitten

Holly Webb
Illustrated by Sophy Williams

LiTTLE TiGER

LONDON

For Rose

LITTLE TIGER
An imprint of Little Tiger Press Limited
1 Coda Studios, 189 Munster Road, London SW6 6AW

Imported into the EEA by Penguin Random House Ireland,
Morrison Chambers, 32 Nassau Street, Dublin D02 YH68

www.littletiger.co.uk

A paperback original
First published in Great Britain in 2025

Text copyright © Holly Webb, 2025
Illustrations copyright © Sophy Williams, 2025
Author photograph © Lou Abercrombie

ISBN: 978-1-78895-739-7

MIX
Paper | Supporting
responsible forestry
FSC
www.fsc.org   FSC® C171272

The Forest Stewardship Council® (FSC®) is a global, not-for-profit
organization dedicated to the promotion of responsible forest management
worldwide. FSC® defines standards based on agreed principles for
responsible forest stewardship that are supported by environmental, social,
and economic stakeholders. To learn more, visit www.fsc.org

10 9 8 7 6 5 4 3 2 1

Chapter One

Hana leaned against her mama's shoulder and watched the lights flicker by as the car sped along. She could hear her little brother Zahir making snuffling noises in his sleep, and wished that she could sleep so easily. But everything was too strange and scary for sleeping. Hana felt as if she needed to keep watch all the time, just in case

something bad was about to happen
to Zahir, or her parents. Her baba was
in the front seat, next to the driver.
Hana could tell Baba was trying hard
to remember his English words, so he
could answer the friendly questions the
driver kept asking – Mark, that was it.
The driver was called Mark.

It had all happened so fast – the
sudden goodbye to the friends they'd
made in the camp in Iraq, the bumpy
ride to the airport, and then the flight.
It was a good thing, of course, that
they'd come here to Britain. But Hana
was used to living in the camp. She had
friends there! She felt as if she knew
everyone and she knew what the days
would bring. Now everything had
changed.

Baba had said that this was what they'd been waiting for – a whole new start in a different country. Hana could go to a real school. He and Mama could get jobs. After a while, they would hopefully be able to have a home of their own that would be a safe place to stay. Hana had tried to imagine it, but it was so hard.

Their real home was in a village in Syria, but they'd had to leave quickly, after the village was overrun by fighters and it was too dangerous for them to stay – that had been two years ago, when Hana was seven and Zahir was a tiny baby. Hana and her family had been living in the camp ever since. She could hardly remember the village they'd left behind – only flashes of memory every so often.

"Who is he?" she whispered to Mama in Arabic, nodding at Mark. The man had been so smiley and kind when he met them at the airport, and now he was driving them somewhere, but Hana didn't really understand what was happening.

"He's a – a volunteer," Mama explained. "Someone kind who wants to help us. There's a group of people in this country, organized by a charity – they offer rooms in their houses to people who've had to leave their homes, like us. Mark is driving us to his house."

"So we're going to live with him?" Hana peered at Mark. She couldn't see very much of him in the dark car, though.

"And his family. Do you remember, at the airport he told us that he had a son about the same age as you?"

"Yes…" Hana said slowly. She hadn't really been listening, the airport had been so overwhelming. The bright lights, all those crowds of people, the announcements in English that she almost understood, but not quite… Hana had stood there, blinking, clinging on to Mama with one hand and her little purple-and-silver backpack with the other. She couldn't let go of her bag – it was the only thing she had from her life in Syria. Even the clothes she'd been wearing when they left the village were gone now – she'd grown out of them so quickly and they'd been passed on and swapped with other families in the camp.

"Oscar," she whispered to Mama. "He's called Oscar."

"That's right!" Mark called from the front of the car. "He's nine, Hana, just like you! He's looking forward to meeting you!"

Hana looked worriedly up at Mama. She'd understood nine – she knew it was her age, she'd learned English numbers in the school at the camp. She could speak quite a lot of English words and phrases now, but she didn't understand well enough to follow Mark's fast speech. He had a kind voice, though. She did her best to reply, murmuring, "Thank you," hoping it was the right thing to say. She knew it was polite.

Mama squeezed her hand, and Baba looked round at her, smiling and nodding. "Good! Use your English!" He and Mama had tried to help Hana learn English too – they'd been hoping that they would be able to travel to Britain one day. She wondered if Oscar would know any Arabic words. Perhaps she could just ask him to speak slowly.

"This is our road," Mark said, turning into a side street.

Hana peered up at the tall houses – there were still a few golden-lighted windows and she could see figures moving behind them, and people talking. There was so much space. The houses had little gardens in front of them, with trees and bushes, or cars parked. She was used to tiny homes built out of concrete blocks, squashed up close together to fit as many people into the overcrowded camp as possible. These houses looked beautiful, but strange – even frightening.

Mark drew up outside one of the tall houses and Hana stared anxiously out of the car window. She spotted a small face looking back at her, peering round the edge of the curtain in an upstairs room.

"It's late," Mark said to her slowly as he turned off the engine. "Oscar is asleep in bed, but he'll be happy to see you tomorrow."

Hana nodded. She'd mostly understood that! Then she glanced up again and saw the curtain drop back.

She had a feeling that actually Oscar
was wide awake and watching.

The calico kitten woke up, blinking
sleepily. She was slumped half on top
of her mother, with her ginger brother's
chin resting on her head. He was warm
but heavy, and the kitten wriggled a
little and mewed crossly when she
couldn't shift him. Her mother leaned
over and gently nudged the ginger
kitten away. He didn't even wake up,
just slid bonelessly over to land with all
four paws pointing up in the air.

The calico kitten yawned and looked
blearily around. Something had woken
her, but she wasn't sure what it was.

She wasn't hungry – she'd fed well a short while before and she didn't want any more milk. Not for a little while, anyway…

Voices echoed outside the door and the kitten pricked up her ears, listening. The house felt different tonight, strange and waiting. But her mother was still stretched out sleepily in their pen, so the kitten was curious rather than frightened. If there was something wrong, their mother would be standing in front of them, her fur fluffed out. She'd be making those little hissing growls that meant she was scared for her babies.

The kitten squeaked in surprise as her mother leaned over and picked her up with a gentle mouth. She

wanted all her kittens close. The calico
kitten purred faintly as her mother
began to wash the top of her head,
licking her fur down flat. The kitten's
head nodded with every swipe of her
mother's tongue. She yawned again
and snuggled close against the mother
cat's fluffy white front.

Everything was fine. Everyone was
safe. She was going back to sleep.

Chapter Two

Mark and his wife Carla had explained that they only had one spare room, so Hana's family would all have to sleep together. They apologized and said they wished they had more space, but Hana thought the room was lovely. Even last night, when she was feeling so tired and overwhelmed, she'd noticed the big bed for her parents, with a comfy folding bed for her set at the end. There was a cot for Zahir in the corner, but Hana wasn't sure if he would use it since he was used to sleeping cuddled up to Mama. So was she – but the camp bed looked so nice with the bright pink-and-white stripey covers. There was even a set of new clothes to sleep in. Mama had seen them and started to cry, and then she'd hugged Carla and Carla had cried too.

Hana sat up in the camp bed, looking around the room in the faint light that filtered through the curtains. Her purple backpack was still safe at the end of her bed. Her most precious things were in there, the little plastic pony that she kept in the front pocket, and the pretty red bracelet that her tete, her mother's mother, had given her, along with a few clothes.

Baba and Mama were still asleep, but Zahir was sitting up between them, sucking his thumb, his dark eyes wide and worried. He looked relieved when he saw that Hana was awake, and wriggled out of the covers and down the bed towards her. Hana put out her arms and they cuddled close, holding each other silently. Hana could hear sounds downstairs – music playing and people talking. A door banged and then Hana felt her mouth lift in a tiny smile. That noise – was it a mew? She was almost sure she'd heard a cat.

There had been cats in the refugee
camp. Thin, hungry creatures, most
of them, too intent on hunting the
rats and mice to want to play or be
petted. But the family who lived in
the little shelter next door to Hana's
had somehow managed to bring their
own ginger cat Jabir with them, tucked
safely away in a basket when they fled
their home. Maritza, her friend from

next door, had let Hana play with him sometimes. Once Jabir had even fallen asleep in Hana's lap, and she'd sat, frozen, listening in wonder to his faint purring snores. She still loved to remember it, the softness of his fur under her fingers.

She hadn't known that Mark and Carla had a cat, she must have been too sleepy to notice the night before.

"Shall we get up?" she whispered to Zahir in Arabic. "We could go and see that cat?"

"Cat!" Zahir agreed happily.

Hana knew they should probably wait for Baba and Mama to wake up, but she was twitchy and nervous and didn't want to stay quietly waiting in their room. Waves of excitement and fear kept washing over her, one after the other. She couldn't keep still. She wanted to meet that boy who'd been peeping round the curtains. And the cat – she wanted to meet the cat even more.

Hana eased the bedroom door open and shushed Zahir as they crept out on to the landing. It had a set of wooden rails that they could look through down the stairs into the hallway. Hana leaned over the top rail, and Zahir stuck his nose between the wooden bars. They could hear voices, and then there was a click and a burst of music as a door opened. Hana drew back quickly as a boy about her own age came running up the stairs. He wasn't looking at the landing above his head,

so he swung round the banister and
nearly bumped into Hana and Zahir.

"Oh!" He stopped himself, staring at
them both. "You're awake."

Hana nodded,
suddenly
speechless.
What was she
supposed to say?
She couldn't
remember
any English
words. Even
in Arabic, she
wasn't sure what
to say to the person whose house she
was now living in.

"Thank you…" she mumbled
eventually.

The boy – Oscar, that was it – put his head on one side, looking puzzled. "What for?"

Hana blinked at him and translated in her head. "Good room?"

"You like it? Mum spent ages trying to work out how to fit the cot in. It's a bit squashed. Do you want some breakfast?"

Hana missed most of that but latched on to breakfast. She was so hungry, and she was sure Zahir was too.

"Yes! Breakfast, thank you."

Oscar nodded, looking pleased. "Come on." He beckoned them back down the stairs, and then reached out a hand to help Zahir. Hana expected her little brother to pull away, but instead he began chattering cheerfully to Oscar as the older boy edged backwards down the stairs, holding his hand. She followed them, wondering what there could be for breakfast. Baba and Mama had warned her that the food might be very different here, but she was hungry enough to eat anything.

"They're awake!" Oscar called as he led Zahir through the kitchen door. "They want breakfast, can I have second breakfast?"

Hana smiled shyly at Carla – the lovely person who had bought her pyjamas and the pretty bedding – the person whose house they were living in. Hana felt grateful but almost embarrassed too. She didn't think she would know what to say to Carla even in Arabic, and she certainly didn't have the words in English. All she could do was smile.

Carla beamed back. She started pulling things out of cupboards and a tall fridge in the corner of the room, showing them to Hana to see if she and Zahir would like to eat them. Mark showed Hana and Zahir the toasted bread he was eating, but Hana wasn't sure about the strange brown spread he'd put on it. She was just nodding eagerly at a tub of yogurt and some sweet fruit jam to go on the top, when a tiny squeak from the other side of the kitchen made her swing round. The room was huge, with a big table in the middle and a door out to the garden – but she hadn't noticed there was another door too, leading to a smaller room.

"Cat?" she whispered to Oscar, remembering the mewing. She couldn't quite see – it looked like there was a sort of cage in the room. Did people keep cats in cages here?

"Yes." Oscar nodded wildly. "Cat! Mum, can I show them the kittens?"

"Sure, just be careful not to upset Rose – you know she's still shy."

Oscar beckoned, but then put his finger to his lips, and whispered,

"Sshhhh!" He led them across the kitchen on exaggerated tiptoes, which was so funny that Zahir giggled and followed him, trying to do it too. Hana glanced back at Carla, confused, but Carla smiled and nodded at her.

"It's OK. Go and see!"

There was washing hanging up in the little room, and a washing machine – and in the corner was the cage, except it wasn't really a cage, Hana saw now, it was more like a circle of wire mesh. Inside it, snoozing on a pile of soft blankets, were four tiny kittens and their mother, a large black cat with long, soft-looking fur.

The mother cat woke up as she heard Zahir's delighted giggling and glared at the three children.

"She's shy," Oscar said, pointing at her. He crouched down next to Zahir and said, "Shhhh. Gentle…"

Hana was just sorting out the words in her head to try and explain that Zahir didn't know any English – he didn't know that many words in Arabic either, he was only two – when her little brother nodded seriously and echoed, "Shhhh." He sat down in front of the wire mesh pen and babbled quietly at the mother cat, who seemed to relax a little. She was still watching them all suspiciously, but she didn't get up and she didn't hiss at them, the way the half-wild cats at the camp had sometimes.

"Her name is Rose," Oscar said slowly. "Rose. Yes?"

"Rose," Hana repeated, nodding eagerly. "Babies?" she added.

"Uh-huh. Kittens. Babies." Oscar smiled at her, and Hana smiled back.

Zahir let out a little yelp of excitement, and Hana realized that one of the kittens had woken up. There were four of them – two ginger and white, one black, and one kitten who looked as if she'd started off white but had been splattered with orange and black paint so only her white paws and white front were left. She had been stretched out fast asleep on her mother's back, but Rose's worried twitching when the children arrived had obviously woken her up. Now she gave a huge yawn, showing teeny white points of teeth and a long bright pink tongue, and opened her eyes, which were a soft, deep blue.

Hana sucked in a delighted breath. She'd never seen such a beautiful cat.

The kitten yawned, then stared curiously at the three children gazing

at her through the wire mesh. She
knew Oscar, of course. He often
brought the kittens their food, and
Rose let him stroke them and even
pick them up sometimes. But the other
two were new. Slowly, she wriggled
and half tumbled down into the nest of
blankets, and set off to investigate.

"She's coming to see you!" Oscar said proudly, nudging Hana's arm.

The kitten stumbled over the blankets to the edge of the pen, and put her nose against the small boy's fingers, making him coo and giggle.

Oscar picked her up, and she snuggled against his T-shirt, watching as the other two children stared.

"You can stroke her," he told them slowly, and the littlest child said, "Shhhh. Gen-tle," and reached out, running one tiny finger down the kitten's back. The girl tickled the kitten under her chin, murmuring delightedly at the feel of the soft fur. The kitten licked the back of her hand, and saw the girl's eyes widen in surprise as she began to purr.

Chapter Three

When Baba and Mama came downstairs
at last, looking dazed and full of
apologies for sleeping in, Hana felt
she couldn't possibly catch them up on
everything that had happened. There
were kittens, not just a cat, and they
belonged to Oscar's family, and they were
so beautiful and sweet and tame, and
Zahir had said a new word, in English!

Hana wanted to know all the cats' names, but Oscar and his mum and dad explained that the kittens weren't named yet.

"They're four weeks old but we still haven't decided. Dad keeps making up weird ones for them," Oscar said, rolling his eyes.

"Weird…?" Hana shook her head helplessly.

"Um … silly? Funny? He keeps calling the ginger kitten Nigel, or Trevor!"

Hana shook her head. "Not a good name?"

"No!" Oscar shook his head wildly, and his dad chuckled.

"That kitten looks like a Trevor to me. Did you tell Hana why Rose is called Rose?"

Hana frowned, working through this in her head. "Why?" she asked, and Mark gave her a thumbs up. She knew what that meant. He was pleased with her.

"We found her under a rose bush in the garden. She was looking for somewhere safe to have her babies. We spotted her one morning, just sitting there, and she was still there that night. Mum posted on all the local groups, asking if anyone had lost her, but she was really thin, apart from her tummy where the kittens were. She didn't look like anyone had been feeding her. I'll show you, look!" Oscar went over to the back door, beckoning Hana to follow him.

"She hasn't got shoes on!" Carla pointed out.

"I can show her from the door. Here,

Hana, do you see? This bush, it has flowers called roses? Like Rose the cat? And – " he beamed at her – "it's prickly." He ran over to the bush – he didn't have shoes on either, but his mum hadn't noticed – and pressed his finger to the stems, miming that it hurt and making an *ouch* face. Then he hurried back into the kitchen and stood by the door to Rose's room, pointing at her.

"I don't understand." Why did spiky thorns on the rose bush mean Rose was a good name for a cat?

"Because Rose the cat is prickly! It means – um – fierce! Grumpy!" Oscar added sound effects to help. "*Grrrrr, hisssss?*" Zahir stared at him worriedly, but Carla guided him back to the sweet yogurt.

"Ohhhh." Hana thought she understood.

"Rose isn't really fierce," Carla said. "She's scared. She's a stray cat, so she doesn't really know much about people. But she understands that we want to help – at least, I think she does." She sighed, and then smiled at Hana, who nodded back.

Carla and Mark and Oscar had

taken Rose in and given her a home, and food, and a safe place to look after her babies – a bit like they had for Hana and her family. Hana could understand why Rose was still feeling scared and shy about it all. Everything was so different. She felt just the same way.

"You could name her, if you wanted?" Oscar said, nodding at the multi-coloured calico kitten, who was climbing slowly but steadily up the leg of Hana's trousers. "My mum and dad said that I could choose what they were called. I don't mind if you want to pick."

"Oh…" Hana looked down at the tiny kitten, who had finally managed to scramble into her lap. The calico cat gazed around, her head nodding wearily, and then slumped down, her chin resting on Hana's sweater.

Her family had been here for three days now – today was the first day that Oscar had gone to school. He had done his best to look after her and Zahir all through the weekend, and Hana had missed him more than she thought she would, even if she only understood about half of what he was saying – he was so friendly. And she was getting better at understanding. Oscar was good at pointing at things and acting out what he meant.

He'd left her with some colouring

books and felt tips that morning, and Carla had given her some books to help her practise reading English. Hana was a lot better at speaking English than she was at reading or writing it, and she'd have to do both when she went to school too. Mark and Carla and her parents were trying to arrange for her to go to Oscar's school, but it would take a few days to sort out, they said. Hana was determined to practise as much as she could before then. Oscar had got out some of his old toys for Zahir as well. The kittens had enjoyed exploring a tower that Zahir and Mama had built of Duplo that morning. Rose had been a bit suspicious about it, though.

"I will think about a name. Thank you." Hana found herself blinking to get tears out of her eyes. Naming the kitten was special. It seemed to mean that she belonged. She would have to find just the right name. Hana looked down at the kitten, who had fallen asleep in seconds. She could just see the fur ruffling gently with her tiny breaths. What would be the perfect name for her? Should she give her a British name, because they were here now? The kitten had been born here too. But Hana hadn't. Maybe she should give the kitten a name that would remind her of home.

Hana swallowed. Mama and Baba wanted her to think of Britain as home now, and for a moment, when Oscar had said she could choose a name, she had almost believed it. But only almost.

"Was school good?" she asked Oscar, trying to change the subject, and Oscar looked at her with his head on one side.

"Do you want to go to school?"

Hana shrugged. "Yes? But I am – scared?"

"Everyone will be nice. We have new people coming all the time in our class. Maxim started last term, he's from Ukraine. His English is really good now, and he hardly knew any when he started. You'll be fine."

"I will miss the kittens," Hana said, gently stroking the top of the calico kitten's head.

"I missed them today," Oscar agreed. "I think they've grown while I've been at school. Her eyes are changing colour too – they're definitely more green than blue today."

Hana peered down to see, but the kitten's eyes were firmly closed, and there was no way she was going to wake her up to check.

The kitten stretched, her tiny, pin-thin claws hooking into the fabric of Hana's sweater. She padded her paws up and down for a moment, and then licked them sleepily. Then she sat up, balancing carefully on the shifting sweater. She could feel Hana breathing underneath her.

"Yes! Green – they are green. I didn't see."

"I think I only noticed because I didn't see her all day." Oscar sighed.

"So pretty," Hana murmured, gently scratching the kitten under her chin. "What we call you, hmmm?"

The kitten gazed back at her with huge, round eyes – now definitely more green than blue – and then butted her head against Hana's hand. She let out a loud kitten mew, one that meant she was hungry and she'd like Hana to do something about it.

"She wants milk?" Hana asked Oscar.

"Put her back?" She waved at the pen, where Rose was watching them carefully.

"Yeah, I think so."

The kitten squeaked again as Hana stood up. She was swaying, but safely held in Hana's cupped hands. She waved her paws wildly as Hana laid her back in among the soft blankets next to her mother. Her sister and two brothers were waking up now too, and the kitten bustled her way as fast as she could to her mother's side, so as not to miss out.

"Look at her! She's so bossy!" she heard Oscar say as she latched on and started to feed. "She's not letting the others get in her way."

"I know her name," Hana said

slowly as the kitten gulped down her milk, her green eyes blissfully closed. "Amal. It means dreams and – and hope. A hope kitten." Amal meant wishing too, and trust. Someone called Amal would believe that everything was going to be all right. Hana wanted to be just like her.

Chapter Four

Amal purred as Hana crouched down by the pen, murmuring to her through the wire mesh. She stomped determinedly over to nose at Hana, and Hana giggled.

"Kisses…"

Hana's mama came to sit next to her, and Amal nudged at her too. She didn't know the lady as well as Hana and Oscar, but Mama was friendly, and sometimes brought the kittens food. They were eating kitten food now, as well as feeding from Rose. Amal nibbled at Mama's fingers hopefully, in case she might be about to feed them again.

"Sweet kitten," Mama said, and then, "Are you ready, Hana? Time we go."

"Now?" Hana sounded nervous, and Amal flattened her ears a little. What was happening?

"Baba and I are coming too. You will have Oscar, remember. No need to be scared."

"I'm not scared! Just … a bit worried," Hana admitted as she stood up.

"Your English is good now, *habibti*. I'm so proud of you."

Hana hugged Mama, and then leaned over the pen to stroke Amal. "Bye, kitten," she whispered. "I will see you this afternoon. Wish me all the best."

Oscar had told Hana so much about school, and she had been with Mark to pick him up a few times. She'd

even spoken to Oscar's teacher –
her teacher too, now – when he
brought her over to say hello in the
playground.

Hana had told herself that she
didn't need to be nervous. She knew
what school was going to be like!
She'd been to school before, after
all. But she hardly remembered the
school back in her village, and the
school at the refugee camp had been
a tiny building. Everyone went in
shifts, since only a few of the children
could fit in there at a time. It was
nothing like this swirling mass of
people hanging up their coats and
talking about their weekends and – in
one case – turning a cartwheel down
the middle of the corridor. Although

they got told off and sent to the back of their class's line to walk in, so that probably wasn't something that happened often.

"Mrs Foster said you can sit by me," Oscar told her reassuringly as they waited outside the Year Four classroom.

Hana nodded. She could hear some of the girls in the line behind them talking about her. They were whispering, and speaking fast, so Hana wasn't sure what they were saying, but it made her feel prickly like Rose. It wasn't really school that she was worrying about, she realized. It was getting used to all these new people – and them getting used to her.

But one of the girls smiled at her as
they walked into the classroom, and
the boy and girl who sat on the other
side of the table from her and Oscar
were friendly. The boy was called Sam,
and the girl was Isla, they told her.
There would be lots of people to help
her out, they promised. Sam had been
one of the pupils who'd helped look

after Maxim when he first joined.

"Mrs Foster told us last week that you were coming, she showed us how to say some words in Arabic." He reached into a box in the middle of the table and riffled through a set of cards with pictures and Arabic words on, and how they sounded for an English person to say. *Library*, Hana spotted, and *play*. "Oh! I forgot. We all learned to say *Ahlan* to you – it's up on the board over there, look." He pointed to a display that said "Welcome" and "Hello" in lots of different languages. "*Ahlan!*" he added, grinning, and Isla said it too.

"*Ahlan wa salan*," Hana said, smiling. "Means also welcome. Thank you."

Baba and Mama had already
explained to Hana that there would be
a translator coming into class to help
her some of the time, and some of her
lessons would be with other children
who spoke Arabic. No one wanted
Hana to forget her first language while

she was trying so hard to get better at English. But it was so nice to have the other children speaking Arabic to her too – even if it was only a few words.

Over the next couple of weeks, Hana settled into school, and her after-school sessions with other children from Syria who lived around the city. She seemed to be busy all the time, so it was good to come back to Oscar's house to relax and play with Zahir and Oscar and the kittens. They were getting so much bigger and braver. Hana agreed with Oscar – the kittens were definitely growing while they were at school. They came home one

afternoon to find
Amal balanced,
teetering, at the
top of the wire
mesh of the pen.
She was obviously
deciding whether or
not to go for it and jump.

"How did you get up there?" Hana
asked, once she had Amal safely
snuggled up against her school jumper.
"You can climb now!"

"Maybe they're getting too big for
the pen," Oscar suggested. "Mum,
Amal was climbing out of the kitten
pen!"

"Oh, my goodness…" Carla hurried
in, and everyone watched as the biggest
ginger kitten – who *was* called Trevor

now, because even though Oscar had said it was a silly name, it just suited him – started to follow Amal slowly up the side of the pen. "They're all at it! Maybe it's time to get rid of the pen and just put that old baby gate on the kitchen door?"

They'd already been letting Rose out of the little utility room and into the kitchen – and out into the garden for some exploring time away from her kittens, although she never went very far. Now the four kittens were free-range too, and they were everywhere. Both families were constantly tripping over them, and Zahir spent most of his time sitting on the kitchen floor with at least one kitten asleep on top of him. They seemed to think he was just a big kitten toy.

The baby gate in the kitchen wasn't much harder to climb over than the pen had been, and after a couple of days there were kittens all over downstairs. Luckily the tricky height of the steps and the baby gate that was already there for Zahir had kept them from trying to explore upstairs. Hana could just imagine Amal trying to climb the stairs like a mountain. The calico kitten didn't seem to be scared of *anything*. She kept disappearing, because she was convinced that the whole house belonged to her and was there to be climbed over and into and under.

Luckily, she was very hungry too, and always came back for meals, so she didn't usually stay lost for long.

Amal sat on the bottom step of the stairs, just below the stair gate. She'd been nosing at it, trying to work out if she could wriggle round the side and go exploring up there. Hana was always going upstairs. The other three kittens – Trevor and Catkin and Sam – didn't seem to mind, but Amal was curious. She wanted to see. She wanted to know.

The gate was still too tricky for her to manage, though. It was made of a sort of shiny, plasticky fabric, and she couldn't get her claws into it to climb up. She'd been trying for ages, and now she was worn out. She nearly curled up and went to sleep there on the stairs, but the hard wooden step wasn't very comfortable so she hopped down and went to look for somewhere cosier.

Just round the side of the staircase was a basket full of piled-up clothes. It was a perfect kitten bed and much easier to climb than the stairs. Amal scrambled up the plastic sides and nudged hopefully at a sweater of Zahir's that was halfway down the pile. She liked the soft, fleecy stuff it was made of. She pushed her nose under, and then stuck a paw in too, and the other paw, and then managed to wriggle her whole self right underneath the jumper, so she was all snuggled in soft, warm fleece. She stretched deliciously, and then curled back up into a tiny ball inside the washing, completely hidden.

Chapter Five

At lunchtime, Hana and Oscar helped to get the kitten food ready – and food for Rose too. She needed to eat lots of meals, since she was still feeding the kittens sometimes and she'd been very thin to start off with. Mark said they were feeding her up, and Hana liked that idea. It sounded like they were filling her up, from her neat black paws upwards.

Rose was already leaning against Oscar's legs, arching her back and rubbing against him. She could smell the food and she knew the sound of the packets opening.

"She's so friendly now," Hana said, laughing as Rose let out a creaky mew.

"She never used to mew like that," Oscar said. "I think she noticed that we make a fuss over the kittens when they mew. She's worked out it's the way to make us listen."

"She's clever." Hana turned round from the counter with the bowl of kitten food and saw three kittens waiting for her eagerly. A black kitten and two ginger and white ones. But no calico.

"Where's Amal?" she asked, looking around the kitchen, expecting Amal to shoot out from under the table or behind the door.

Oscar put Rose's food in front of her and then straightened up. "She'll be here in a minute," he said confidently. "Amal!" He rustled the foil packet that the kitten food had come in, scrunching it in his hand – all the other kittens and Rose looked up hopefully, obviously thinking it meant more food. No calico kitten raced hungrily into the kitchen, though.

After ten minutes of watching the other kittens eat – they had to take some food out of the bowl to save it for Amal – Hana and Oscar were starting to get worried. Hana's mama was searching all the kitchen cupboards, since they'd found Trevor in among the saucepans the day before. Mark was checking the garden, just in case Amal could possibly have sneaked out when he went to cut the grass. They'd taken the kittens outside a couple of times to let them see what the garden was like, but they didn't go out on their own yet.

Hana and Oscar wandered anxiously around the kitchen and the living room and the hallway, lifting things up – silly things, like shoes. They knew that Amal was far too big to fit in a shoe these days, although she could probably have squeezed into one of Baba's shoes when Hana and her family first arrived. But they were getting desperate.

"Where can she be?" Hana said miserably as they both came back into the hallway. "We've looked everywhere."

"I don't think she could have got out at the front of the house," Oscar said, looking doubtfully at the front door.

Hana caught at his sleeve. "Did you hear that? A mew?"

"Wasn't it one of the other kittens in the kitchen?"

"No, upstairs!"

"She's too little to have climbed upstairs – she can't have!" But they both stood on the bottom step, leaning over the stair gate and peering up. And there, at the top of the stairs, was a tiny orange, black and white face, looking back at them halfway up the wooden railings along the landing.

"How did she…" Oscar shook his head and wrenched the stair gate open, racing up the stairs to grab Amal before she toppled through.

Amal wriggled indignantly out of Oscar's hands as he came back down the stairs, squirming over to Hana, who cuddled her, pressing the kitten against her T-shirt. She thought Amal could probably hear her heart beating, it seemed to be thumping so loud. "She's – she's OK."

"I think so. She was standing on top of that basket of washing."

"The washing!" Mama gasped. She'd come up behind them, and they'd been too intent on Amal to notice her. "I took the washing up!" She waved at the stairs. "Amal was in there?"

Oscar nodded. "She must have been – I bet she crawled in and went to sleep, and you didn't see her when you took the box up."

Mama shook her head. "I'm so sorry! Oh, Amal…The fright you gave us." She tickled the kitten behind her ears. "I will tell Mark that she is safe. They are getting so big and brave now, these kittens. Nearly time for them to find their new homes, I think."

She hurried away into the kitchen, and Hana stared after her.

New homes? Oscar and Mark and Carla weren't going to let the kittens stay?

"I thought you knew!" Oscar said, when Hana finally made herself ask him. They were sitting on the floor of the utility room, where the kittens still had a comfy basket. Hana had Amal stretched out asleep along her legs, and Oscar was rolling a little ball for ginger-and-white Trevor. "I wish we could keep them all, but Mum and

Dad say we can't have five cats. We never even meant to have one – Rose just turned up." He sighed. "Mum posted a picture of the kittens online, and said they were nearly ready for new homes. A couple of people are coming to see them next week."

"What about Rose?" Hana whispered.

"I think we're going to keep her. She's got much more friendly now. She even sat on Mum's lap yesterday, and Mum didn't move for ages because she didn't want Rose to get up. That's why your baba picked us up from school!"

Hana almost laughed. She was glad that Rose was going to stay, and it *was* funny, thinking of Rose pinning Carla to the sofa. But Amal! Her beautiful kitten was going to live somewhere else!

"I'm really sorry you didn't know." Oscar looked at her guiltily. "But I'm working on Mum and Dad to let us keep Trevor as well. That's good, isn't it? Dad loves him, it's obvious. He wouldn't have named him if he didn't, don't you think?

Hana nodded. Oscar was right.
A name was special, and precious.
Naming Amal had made her belong
to Hana – and it had meant Hana
belonged to her.

Hana swallowed hard, trying to push
down the angry things she wanted
to say. She was angry with Mark
and Carla and Oscar for letting her
feel like Amal was hers, but mostly
she was angry with herself for not
understanding. She felt stupid.

There was a snuffling noise, and
Amal wriggled and put her head back
in a huge yawn. She turned over, so
she was lying on her back in the dip
between Hana's legs, her paws all
flopped. She looked like a toy kitten,
soft and saggy. Hana blinked back

tears, trying not to imagine her Amal belonging to someone else.

It didn't really matter, she tried to tell herself, it wasn't as if *she* would be living here always. Mama and Baba were hoping to get a place of their own soon. They'd explained it to Hana a few days before, that they weren't going to stay with Carla and Mark and Oscar forever. The same charity that had helped them come to Britain was trying to find them a little house to rent, and Mama was going to be able to work again too. She and Baba were excited, and Hana had liked the idea. She'd miss the kittens so much, she'd thought, especially Amal, but she could still come and visit them. She'd still want to see Oscar as well. She'd imagined popping in every day after school…

Except now Amal wouldn't be there.

Amal padded along the hallway and into the living room, looking for her brother and sister. They had all eaten breakfast together, but then there had been strange people in the house. One of them had picked her up and tried to hold her, but Amal hadn't felt like being held. She'd wriggled and mewed, and the woman had put her down quickly. Amal had stalked away, her tail held high and fluffed out, and after that they'd left her alone.

But now the people had gone,

and Catkin and Sam had gone too. Amal wasn't sure what had happened, but she didn't like it. She wanted to snuggle up against Catkin's black fur. She wanted Sam to lick the top of her head and clean her whiskers. She stood by the front door, sniffing the faint scent of outside that came seeping in underneath, and mewed. Where had they gone?

"You miss them?" Hana crouched down beside her. She wasn't happy, Amal thought. Her voice sounded strange. "I do too. But – they were nice people. Carla knows them, they don't live far from here. She said they're kind, I promise."

Amal rubbed herself against Hana's knees and heard Hana sigh. There was a strange catch in her voice when she went on speaking.

"It'll be your turn soon. You're so beautiful, everyone will want you to be their kitten. Oh, Amal!"

Chapter Six

Baba and Mama had taken Zahir out for a walk – he loved the ducks in the park nearby. They'd wanted Hana to go too, but she just hadn't felt like it. Catkin and Sam had been gone for a few days now and the house felt so much emptier with only two kittens. Hana was used to finding tiny cats everywhere she went.

Mark had told them all at breakfast that morning that someone was coming to see Amal on Sunday. Tomorrow. Hana might only have one more day with her, and she wasn't going to waste any of it going out for walks. Instead, she was lying on the sofa, dancing around a feathery toy for Amal to chase. The kitten was bounding about like a gymnast, flinging herself into the air after the bright feathers.

"Have you done that numeracy homework?" Oscar asked, putting his head round the door. He and Hana didn't always have the same stuff to do for homework, but numbers were something Hana was good at, with a bit of help. "I'm doing it now. Get it out of the way."

Hana shook her head. "I don't want to. I'll do it later." She sounded muffled partly because she was upside down, but her voice was thick and strange because she still kept wanting to cry.

Oscar could tell that she wasn't in a good mood, so he only shrugged. "All right."

"How can he care about doing homework?" Hana muttered to Amal. "Doesn't he understand that you're going tomorrow?" She knew that the people might not want to take Amal straight away – they might not even want her at all – but she was preparing for the worst. It was easier than dragging out a horrible long goodbye.

Amal did another enormous leap and caught the feathers, biting down on them hard and giving them a good shake. She was so funny with a giant rainbow feather moustache that Hana couldn't help laughing. "You look so silly," she told Amal lovingly. "Silly little cat."

Perhaps it was the laugh that shook her out of her miserable darkness. She'd been thinking for days that Amal was going and there was nothing she could do about it. It wasn't up to her, was it? The kittens belonged to Carla and Mark, they could say what was going to happen to them. All she could do was cover Amal in love, so that she would be happy when she went to her new home, but just maybe she'd remember Hana a little bit.

But the laugh – or perhaps it was Amal herself, so brave and fearless with her wild leaps – lit something inside Hana. Did Amal really belong to Mark and Carla? If she belonged to anyone, it was Rose! And Rose would want Amal to stay with Hana, who loved her most of all. Hana was sure about that. Rose quite liked her too now. She let Hana scratch under her chin and snuggle her ears. She even purred for her.

Rose wouldn't want Amal to go away with strangers. She was already confused about Catkin and Sam. She'd searched the house for them, and she'd made an extra fuss of Trevor and Amal, following them round, and even picking up Trevor in her mouth and carrying him back to the basket when she felt he'd gone too far away. He was so much bigger now, she hadn't been able to pick him up properly – his back paws had trailed along the floor as Rose marched him back to the utility room. Hana was watching, and Trevor didn't even mew. He just sagged and let Rose carry him along. Perhaps he felt like being fussed over, if he was missing his brother and sister.

By now, Hana was practically

convinced that Amal belonged with her. She had to take Amal away, before her new owners came to meet her.

She had to do it *now*.

Mama and Baba were out with Zahir. Oscar was doing his homework in the kitchen, with Mark making something for lunch. Carla was at work. No one was watching her, it was the best chance she was going to get. Hana swung herself round and quietly got up from the sofa, trailing the feather toy along the floor behind her. Amal skittered along after it, pouncing on the feathers with excited little jumps. Hana peered round the living-room door – Oscar was concentrating on his homework and Mark was by the oven. Neither of them were watching.

She hurried to the stair gate, opening it as silently as she could, and tempted Amal through with the toy. Then she scooped her up and crept up the stairs. Amal could probably have climbed them by herself – her legs were so much longer now – but it would have been one long, exciting game, bouncing from step to step. Hana didn't have time for that now.

She let herself into their room and sat down on her folding bed, with

Amal in her lap. The kitten looked around curiously – she'd never been in here before, Hana realized. But she didn't try to explore, she was still too interested in the feather toy. She stalked across Hana's lap, batting at it every so often.

It had been clever idea to bring the toy, Hana thought. She hadn't meant to do it, but she needed something to keep Amal occupied. She leaned over carefully and grabbed her purple backpack from under the bed.

The bag had once been packed with her favourite things, a few clothes and some snacks for their journey, but now the main part of it was empty – the toy pony and her little bracelet were still in the front pocket, but Hana's clothes were folded neatly in the chest of drawers behind Zahir's cot. Hana stood up, gently setting Amal on the bed with her toy, and fetched a couple of T-shirts and a hoodie, and a pair of tracksuit trousers. She didn't need much, and she didn't want to fill the bag up, but she did want it to be soft and cosy for Amal. She stuffed them all in and then looked hopefully at the kitten. She'd been playing with that feather toy for ages. Surely she must be getting sleepy by now? And she liked small, cosy places. They'd had all that trouble last week, finding her after she crawled into the washing for a nap.

"Wouldn't you like a little sleep in here?" she suggested hopefully, leaning the open bag towards Amal.

The kitten
glanced over at
it, and then
went back
to hunting
the feathers,
rolling
over on to
her back and
gripping the
toy tightly with
her front paws, growling at it fiercely.

Hana sighed. Amal didn't look
sleepy at all. The kitten wasn't
really interested in anything but
the feathers. Then she had an idea.
Avoiding Amal's tiny but sharp
claws, she picked up the stick end of
the feather toy and poked it down

among the clothes in her backpack.
The feathers stuck up above her
T-shirt, and Amal bounced along the
bed after them. She sat up on her
hind paws, batting at them as they
poked out through the zip, and then
she didn't seem to mind when Hana
gently boosted her into the bag too.

Hana laughed. The bag and the
bracelet and the little pony – and now
Amal. All her most special things
together. Now all she had to do was
steal them away.

She pulled the zip closed, whispering
gently to Amal, and she'd just picked
the bag up to put it on her shoulder
when suddenly it shook. There was
a frantic mewing from inside, and a
scrabbling sound. And then a rip –

those sharp kitten claws were tearing
at the worn purple fabric. Hana yelped.
Her bag! Her precious bag!

"Amal, no!" Hana dropped the bag
back on the bed, her hands shaking as
she tried to undo the zip again.

"What are you doing? You're hurting
her! Get her out of there!"

Hana hadn't even noticed Oscar
come in – he never usually came into
the room without being asked, but he
must have heard Amal mewing.

"I'm not hurting her, I'm trying
to get her out!" Hana snapped. Her
backpack was ruined – Amal was going
to shred it with her claws. She got the
zip half undone, and a little black and
orange head popped out, hissing with
fury.

"Look at her," Oscar shouted angrily.
"Her fur's all on end! What were you
doing, trying to shut her in a bag?" He
snatched at it, tearing the zip out of
Hana's grasp and dragging it all the

way open – but the zip pull came off in his hands as the frightened kitten leaped out of the backpack and dived under the bed.

Chapter Seven

Amal darted underneath the folding bed, and then into the shadows under the bigger bed, scrabbling her way between boxes and bags. Her fur was all ruffled up, and her tail was fluffed out as far as it would go.

She *did* like small spaces – but only if she chose them. She hadn't wanted to be shut up in that bag. It had been all right with the zip open – the bag smelled like Hana, and she'd wanted to keep chewing on those feathers. But when Hana did up the zip, she'd suddenly felt trapped and terrified. She'd yowled and clawed, and the backpack had swung around, and then Oscar and Hana were shouting…

It had been horrible. She was going to find her own small safe space now. Somewhere quiet and dark. She wanted to watch and listen and lick her paws and wash her ears until she felt better. The angry voices were still echoing above her. And then she heard running footsteps and the bang of a door. There was a muffled clanging from the stair gate, and then quiet.

A sigh.

A thump as someone sat down on the floor beside the bed.

"Amal…" That was Oscar, still sounding upset. Amal wriggled further back among the boxes. She didn't want to be near either of the children, not yet. She'd heard them arguing before, occasionally, and she'd heard Zahir crying, but this had been different. She'd been *frightened*.

"I bet you don't want to come out." Oscar sighed again. "I wouldn't either. I'm sorry, Amal. I shouldn't have grabbed the bag like that – but you were screeching and I was scared. Hana's so upset with me now. I broke the zip… I don't know what to do."

His voice was quiet and soothing, even though it sounded sad. Amal crept a little closer.

"What are we going to do?"

Amal peered out of the shadows, watching the boy as he leaned back against the wall. He picked up the purple bag, and she shivered, remembering trying to fight her way out. He turned it over and over in his hands, fiddling with the zip, and then shook his head. "It's bust," he muttered. "Maybe Mum could fix it?"

Amal edged a little closer, peering out under the trailing edge of the duvet. Oscar wasn't shouting now. He was quiet, and still, and peaceful. She forgot to be scared. She padded out from beneath the bed and sniffed at his bare toes so that he giggled and twitched, then squeaked as she tried to pounce on his feet.

"Don't eat my toes! Ow, stop nibbling, Amal." He picked her up gently and sat her on his lap, running one hand down her back over and over, smoothing her fur so nicely. It had been dusty under the bed. Amal stretched and relaxed, settling into the folds at the front of his T-shirt, and starting to purr sleepily. She was worn out from all that feather chasing, and then the strange, frightening argument. Oscar didn't stroke her quite as well as Hana did, but he would do. She stuck her head up into the air and waited for him to scratch her under the chin.

Now if only Hana would come back too…

Hana raced downstairs, fighting with the stair gate, and then ran through the kitchen and out into the back garden. She heard Mark start to say something behind her, but she didn't stop to listen. She wanted to get away from all of them.

How could she have thought she was going to run away with Amal? Looking back on it now, Hana couldn't believe she'd tried to hide the kitten in her backpack. Where did she think she was going? She knew her school, the park, the community centre where she did her classes. The cinema they'd all gone to for a treat. What was she going to do – run away and live in the little hut at the top of the climbing frame in the playground?

She hadn't thought about it properly

at all – she hadn't thought any further than getting Amal out of the house. She'd been so desperate, she had made herself believe it would work. It had seemed perfectly sensible at the time. But now she could see there was nothing she could do to stop Amal being taken away.

Hana curled herself up into a ball under the rose bushes, buried her face in her arms, and wept.

"Hana…"

Hana sniffled and wriggled around, turning her back on Oscar.

"Hana, you've got to help, I can't hold on to them both!"

She looked back over her shoulder, and gasped – Oscar had both kittens, Trevor and Amal, tucked up in his arms. They obviously wanted to explore the garden, and they were wriggling. Oscar was struggling to keep hold.

"You shouldn't have brought them out here!" she said, her voice hoarse with crying, but she stood up and rescued Amal, who was dangling under Oscar's arm.

"Yeah, well, Dad saw you were upset. He told me I should try and cheer you up. He thought the kittens would help. He said he was about to come upstairs because we were shouting, and then you dashed past him in a state."

"I'm not," Hana said proudly, even though she knew he knew she'd been crying.

"I'm sorry I yelled at you. And I'm really sorry I broke your bag. I never meant to do that, I promise."

Hana's mouth twisted and she swallowed hard. She set Amal down on the grass and followed her as she started to explore – that way she didn't have to look at Oscar. "I know you didn't," she muttered.

"What was Amal doing in there anyway?" Oscar had put Trevor down now, and the ginger kitten was following his sister. "I know you didn't mean to hurt her, but you shouldn't have done that, Hana! You must have known she wouldn't like it."

Hana looked back at him properly for the first time, wondering what to say. She and Baba and Mama were so grateful to Oscar and his family. They'd been so welcoming, so kind. She didn't want to upset him. But she was worn out and miserable, and it just seemed easier to tell him the truth.

"I was going to run away with her," she said quietly.

"What?" Oscar squeaked, and Amal froze, staring at him wide-eyed.

"Shhhh, it's all right," Hana murmured. "She's still upset because we were shouting." She smiled as

Amal turned away and began to sniff curiously at a dandelion.

"You were going to run away? Where to?"

Hana shrugged. "I didn't know. Somewhere no one could take Amal from me. It was not a good plan."

Oscar shook his head slowly. "You – you – wow."

Hana sighed. "It was stupid."

"You really don't want her to go," Oscar said softly.

"We are going too." Hana sighed. "One day soon, Mama and Baba say. They hope."

"I know." Oscar picked Trevor up, cuddling the ginger kitten close. "I'll really miss you."

"Me too. But I will see you at

school!" Hana leaned over to dance a long grass stem for Amal to chase – and because she didn't want to look at Oscar and think about the way everything was going to change.

But if she had looked at him, she'd have seen him frowning thoughtfully at her and Amal. As if he was starting to make a plan.

Amal flopped on to the grass, wriggling blissfully as she felt the warmth of the sun on her tummy. She'd only been outside a few times, but she loved the smells, the different feels under her paws. She caught a faint twitch of movement and rolled on to her side, fascinated by an earwig, tracking slowly through the grass.

She still didn't understand what had happened earlier on. Why Hana had tried to shut her up in a bag. She could tell that there was something that was making Hana upset – it half frightened Amal, and half made her want to climb up Hana's legs. She needed to pin the girl down and lick her face and knead on her tummy with loving, comforting paws.

The earwig disappeared under a leaf and Amal stood up, stalking back to Hana and Oscar with her tail waving proudly. She walked between them, rubbing the side of her head against their legs and purring as loudly as she could. She wanted to tell them that she loved them. That they were hers.

Chapter Eight

Hana zipped up the purple backpack
– carefully. Mama and Carla between
them had mended it, taking out the
old broken zip and stitching in a
new one, but the fabric was fragile.
The bag needed to be looked after.
Mama had said that at the new flat,
perhaps, it should live on a shelf and
be for looking at, not for using. For

now, Hana had put some books and colouring pens in it. She had a new cat colouring book that Oscar had given her to say goodbye, and some books in Arabic that she'd been given from her classes at the community centre. In the purple and silver pocket with her bracelet and the little pony was a tiny photo album, full of pictures of Oscar and Rose and Trevor and Amal – and Mark and Carla too.

She looked around the room one last time as she stood by the door. The folding bed had only a mattress on it now – Carla said she wanted Hana to take the pretty stripey bedding to the new flat, that it was a present. The room looked strange, empty and bare, but they'd been so happy here.

"Are you ready?" Oscar came along the landing. "Your mama says it's time to go."

"Will you have another family staying in this room?"

Oscar sighed. "I don't know. I suppose so, but it would be really weird – it's your room now."

"You can come and see us in our flat," Hana said hopefully. "It's not far away. It's nice. I have my own bedroom, just for me."

The room was tiny, but it was all hers. Mama said it was important that Hana had a space of her own. There was even a little desk to do her homework, and a window that looked out on to the garden that belonged to the flat – a tiny patch of grass and a paved area with space for flowerpots. Carla had split some of her herbs and planted them up so Mama and Baba could grow their own. They also had a tall rose bush, with a few sweet-smelling yellow roses. Mama said it needed pruning, and maybe some special food – but all Hana could think was that maybe, one day, they'd find a beautiful black cat like Rose hiding underneath it.

"Hana!" That was Mama calling from downstairs. Mark was going to drive them to the new flat with their bags. Hana and Oscar hurried down, and Oscar ran to fetch Trevor and Amal so she could say goodbye. The couple who'd been coming to look at Amal had never turned up. When Hana asked about it – she'd wanted to know what was going to happen, so she could get used to the idea – Carla had just sighed. "I suppose I ought to post more photos of her online. But maybe three cats are

OK? I don't like the idea of someone I don't know taking her. She's such a funny little monster."

Hana had nodded wildly, even though she didn't think Amal was a monster at all. Sometimes Carla didn't say words the way Hana thought they meant. They were keeping her! Amal would get to stay with Rose and Trevor! It was exactly what she'd wanted to happen. Oscar could tell her every day at school what Amal had been up to.

Hana cuddled Amal close, and Oscar held Trevor up to nuzzle at her cheek. Even Rose wandered through from the kitchen. She wound herself round Hana's legs and then let Zahir try to hug her.

"Time to go," Mark murmured at last – but that just meant another round of hugs for everybody.

"Come and visit us," Mama begged Carla. "Let us make you dinner one night next week."

Hana looked back as they got into the car – Oscar and Carla had shut the door to stop the cats running out, but they were standing by the living-room window with Trevor and Rose sitting on the windowsill. Oscar was holding Amal and making her wave a paw.

I'll come back and see them, Hana told herself. *Oscar gave me lots of photos. The new flat is our own place. Think about having your very own bedroom!*

But it was still so hard to drive
away. Hana leaned against the
window, watching the streets slide by
and remembering that first journey
from the airport, weeks ago.

"Shall we stop for a treat? Maybe

buy a cake, or some ice cream?" Mark suggested from the front. "Something to celebrate your new house?"

Hana blinked, surprised, as the adults agreed, and Mark drew up the car not far from a bakery. She supposed it would be nice to have a special treat in their new home. She chose an iced bun with a cherry on top, and Zahir insisted on an enormous chocolate muffin. Baba and Mama seemed to take ages choosing, so long that Hana thought it was lucky there was no one else in the shop. They bought extra cakes too, murmuring something about having them later. Hana was impatient to get back in the car and reach the flat so she could see her new room again.

Their new street looked beautiful,
Hana thought. There was a tree with
pink blossom not that far from the
flat, and there were little pink petals
scattered along the pavement. Perhaps
there would be more yellow roses in
the garden too. She watched eagerly

as Mama put the key in the door and let them in.

"Hana, you take your things and put them in your room," Baba said, smiling at her and handing her a laundry bag that had her clothes and the stripey bedding. "Then we can make tea, and eat the cakes, mmm?"

Hana nodded. She could look for the roses out of her window, she realized, bumping the big bag down the hallway to the tiny end bedroom. And perhaps she could put her bedding on her new bed – that would make the room feel like it was hers.

But when she opened the door, there was already something on the bed – a small plastic box, with a wire-barred front – and the box was mewing.

Hana stared at it, and everything seemed to slow down. She could hear the mews, and noise from the kitchen – lots of voices. Was that Oscar's voice? But he was back at his house… She didn't understand.

But there really was a cat in that box on her bed. She kneeled on the floor, peering in through the wire door, and Amal looked back at her and mewed even louder. Clearly the kitten wanted Hana to let her out.

"What are you doing here?" Hana whispered, struggling with the catches. She was so confused and delighted and surprised that her fingers were clumsy. Eventually she managed to open the door, and Amal came stomping out on to the bare mattress, purring. She pushed the top of her head against Hana's nose, and Hana could *feel* the purr, so loud that it seemed to echo all through the tiny cat.

The tiny cat who shouldn't be there, but was. In a carrier, in her bedroom.

Hana picked her up with trembling hands and walked back along the passage and into the kitchen. They were all there – Baba and Mama and Zahir, and Carla and Mark and Oscar – beaming at her.

"You didn't guess?" Oscar asked hopefully.

"How did you – you were at your house, and so was Amal…" Hana shook her head. "We had the car?"

Carla laughed. "Oscar and I got a lift from my friend down the road. She thought it was a brilliant plan. You had to stop for cakes to give us a bit of time to get here before you. I had the spare key!"

"I thought it was strange that we stopped!" Hana shook her head, and then laughed as Amal nudged against her chin. "Is she ours?" she asked, wanting to make absolutely sure, to be certain. "We can keep Amal?"

"Our own cat," Mama assured her. "Oscar told us, Hana, that you tried to run away." She pressed her hand against her heart. "Because you hated her to go."

Baba nodded. "This is all our home now."

"We should have seen how much you loved her," Mark said. "We didn't realize."

"It's all right," Hana whispered. Everything was all right, with Amal trying to climb on to her shoulder, nibbling at her hair. She didn't seem to mind that she was in a new place.

She doesn't mind, not if I'm here too.
Hana unwound the kitten from her
hair, and held her close, feeling Amal
start to purr again.

Out now

From MULTI-MILLION best-selling author

Holly Webb

The Hero Puppy

Illustrated by Sophy Williams

Out now

From MULTI-MILLION best-selling author
Holly Webb

The
Determined
Kitten

Illustrated by Sophy Williams

HOLLY
WEBB

Holly Webb started out as a children's
book editor and wrote her first series for
the publisher she worked for. She has been
writing ever since, with over one hundred
and fifty books to her name. Holly lives
in Berkshire, with her husband and three
children. Holly's pet cats are always
nosying around when she is trying
to type on her laptop.

For more information
about Holly Webb visit:

www.holly-webb.com